Catching the
Speedy Thief

Dinosaur Cove™

A Cretaceous Adventure

Dinosaur Cove™

Catching the
Speedy Thief

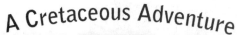

by
REX STONE

illustrated by
MIKE SPOOR

Series created by
Working Partners Ltd

OXFORD
UNIVERSITY PRESS

Special thanks to Jane Clarke

For Guy Macdonald, a true explorer of adventures

OXFORD
UNIVERSITY PRESS

Great Clarendon Street, Oxford OX2 6DP
Oxford University Press is a department of the University of Oxford.
It furthers the University's objective of excellence in research, scholarship,
and education by publishing worldwide in

Oxford   New York

Auckland   Cape Town   Dar es Salaam   Hong Kong   Karachi
Kuala Lumpur   Madrid   Melbourne   Mexico City   Nairobi
New Delhi   Shanghai   Taipei   Toronto

With offices in

Argentina   Austria   Brazil   Chile   Czech Republic   France   Greece
Guatemala   Hungary   Italy   Japan   Poland   Portugal   Singapore
South Korea   Switzerland   Thailand   Turkey   Ukraine   Vietnam

Oxford is a registered trade mark of Oxford University Press
in the UK and in certain other countries

© Working Partners Limited 2008
Illustrations © Mike Spoor 2008

Series created by Working Partners Ltd

Dinosaur Cove is a registered trademark of Working Partners Ltd

The moral rights of the author have been asserted

Database right Oxford University Press (maker)

First published 2008
First published in this edition 2013

British Library Cataloguing in Publication Data

Data available

ISBN: 978-0-19-279369-0

1 3 5 7 9 10 8 6 4 2

Printed in Italy

Paper used in the production of this book is a natural,
recyclable product made from wood grown in sustainable forests
The manufacturing process conforms to the environmental
regulations of the country of origin

FACT FILE

➡️ JAMIE HAS JUST MOVED FROM THE CITY TO LIVE IN THE LIGHTHOUSE IN DINOSAUR COVE. JAMIE'S DAD IS OPENING A DINOSAUR MUSEUM ON THE BOTTOM FLOOR OF THE LIGHTHOUSE. WHEN JAMIE GOES HUNTING FOR FOSSILS IN THE CRUMBLING CLIFFS ON THE BEACH HE MEETS A LOCAL BOY, TOM, AND THE TWO DISCOVER AN AMAZING SECRET: A WORLD WITH **REAL, LIVE DINOSAURS!** THE BOYS HAVE EXPLORED THE JUNGLE, THE MARSH, AND THE CLIFFS, BUT WHEN THEY SPEND TIME AT THE LAGOON, THEY END UP FISHING FOR TROUBLE!

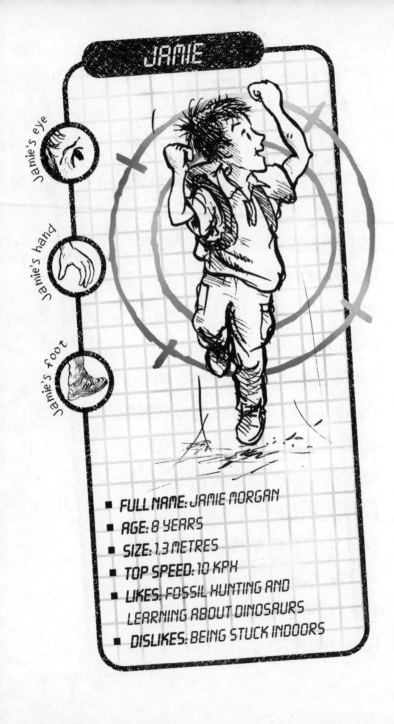

JAMIE

Jamie's eye

Jamie's hand

Jamie's foot

- **FULL NAME:** JAMIE MORGAN
- **AGE:** 8 YEARS
- **SIZE:** 1.3 METRES
- **TOP SPEED:** 10 KPH
- **LIKES:** FOSSIL HUNTING AND LEARNING ABOUT DINOSAURS
- **DISLIKES:** BEING STUCK INDOORS

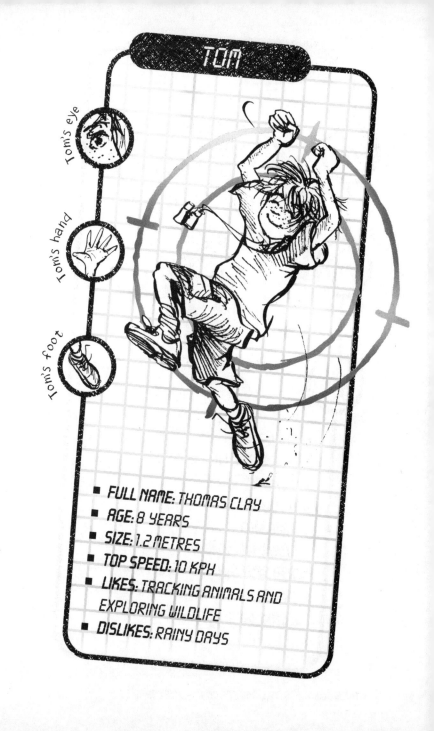

TOM

Tom's eye

Tom's hand

Tom's foot

- **FULL NAME:** THOMAS CLAY
- **AGE:** 8 YEARS
- **SIZE:** 1.2 METRES
- **TOP SPEED:** 10 KPH
- **LIKES:** TRACKING ANIMALS AND EXPLORING WILDLIFE
- **DISLIKES:** RAINY DAYS

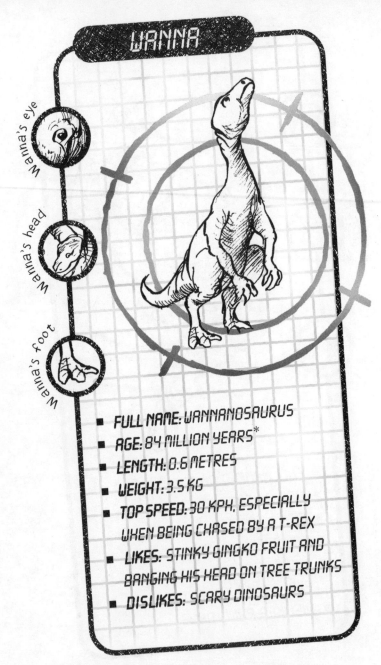

WANNA

Wanna's eye

Wanna's head

Wanna's foot

- **FULL NAME:** WANNANOSAURUS
- **AGE:** 84 MILLION YEARS*
- **LENGTH:** 0.6 METRES
- **WEIGHT:** 3.5 KG
- **TOP SPEED:** 30 KPH, ESPECIALLY WHEN BEING CHASED BY A T-REX
- **LIKES:** STINKY GINGKO FRUIT AND BANGING HIS HEAD ON TREE TRUNKS
- **DISLIKES:** SCARY DINOSAURS

***NOTE:** SCIENTISTS CALL THIS PERIOD THE LATE CRETACEOUS

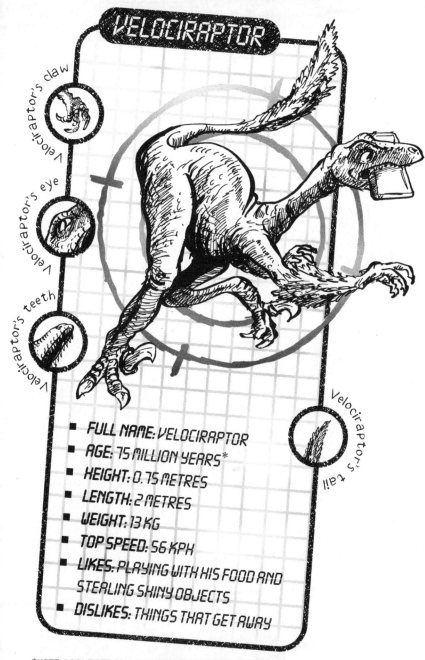

VELOCIRAPTOR

Velociraptor's claw

Velociraptor's eye

Velociraptor's teeth

Velociraptor's tail

- **FULL NAME:** VELOCIRAPTOR
- **AGE:** 75 MILLION YEARS*
- **HEIGHT:** 0.75 METRES
- **LENGTH:** 2 METRES
- **WEIGHT:** 13 KG
- **TOP SPEED:** 56 KPH
- **LIKES:** PLAYING WITH HIS FOOD AND STEALING SHINY OBJECTS
- **DISLIKES:** THINGS THAT GET AWAY

*NOTE: SCIENTISTS CALL THIS PERIOD THE LATE CRETACEOUS

DINOSAUR COVE

Village

Marina

Sealight Head

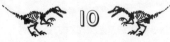

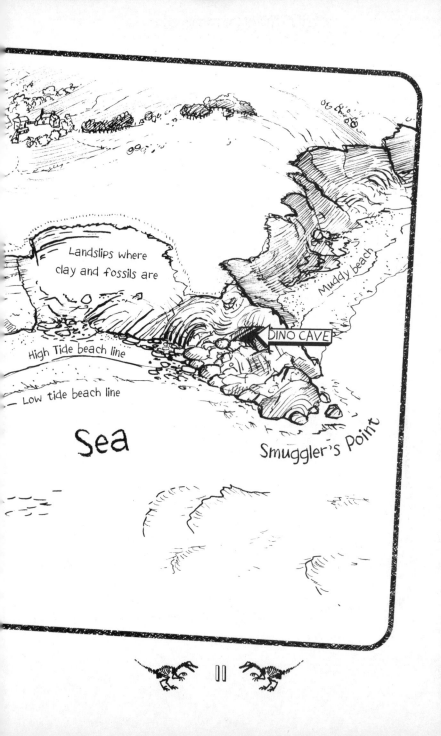

Landslips where clay and fossils are

Muddy beach

DINO CAVE

High Tide beach line

Low tide beach line

Sea

Smuggler's Point

CHAPTER 1

Jamie Morgan pulled a rainbow-coloured metal fish out of his grandad's tackle box and held it up for his friend Tom Clay to see. 'This fish has feathers!' A cluster of tiny

Fisherman's baits

sea bass spinner

crab line

pink and orange feathers sprouted out from where the tail should be.

'Different baits catch different beasts,' Jamie's grandad said with a grin, holding out his hand for the feathery fish. 'This spinner is great for catching sea bass. Now, let's see. What else will I need today?' He tipped a tangle of weights, spinners, and fishing line onto the kitchen floor of the old lighthouse.

'What's this?' Jamie picked up
an H-shaped piece of orange plastic
with string wrapped around it and a
couple of heavy lead weights dangling
from it.

'Haven't you seen one before?'
Tom said in amazement. 'It's a crab
line.'

Jamie shook his head. 'How can
this catch crabs?'

'It's easy,' Tom said. 'You tie a bit
of bacon rind on the end and throw
it in. The crabs grab the bacon and
you grab the crabs!'

'Cool!' said Jamie. 'I'd like to try
that.'

'The best place for crabbing is Sealight Head at high tide,' Grandad said, as he crammed everything but the crab line back in his tackle box. 'But high tide isn't until later this afternoon. I'll meet you there, if you like, after I've caught some sea bass for dinner.'

'OK, Grandad,' Jamie said as the old man

finished packing his tackle box.
'We'll wait until then.'

'We don't have to wait,' Tom whispered to Jamie. 'We could go crabbing in Misty Lagoon in Dino World right now.'

Dino World was Jamie and Tom's secret—even Grandad didn't know that they'd found a world where real live dinosaurs lived.

'Great idea!' Jamie winked at Tom. 'We'll meet you near Sealight Head later, Grandad.'

'Don't forget the bait and mop bucket to put the crabs in,' Grandad told them. He pulled on

17

his fishing boots. 'And I've put two cheese and pickle sandwiches in the fridge for you.' He headed for the door. 'Have fun!'

'We will,' Tom said with a smile. The minute Grandad was out of the door Tom grabbed the handle of the mop bucket. 'Got your Fossil Finder, Jamie?'

'Already in my backpack.' Jamie grinned as he wrapped two cheese and pickle sandwiches in shiny tinfoil and made a separate package for the bacon.

He stuffed them in his
backpack along with the
crab line. 'Let's go!'

The boys clattered
down the stairs of the
lighthouse and dashed
through the dinosaur

exhibits on the ground floor.
Jamie's dad was busy fixing a
label to the wall next to the
triceratops skull.

'How's the museum going, Mr
Morgan?' Tom asked.

'Great, thanks,' said Jamie's dad.
'The Grand Opening is only a few
days away.'

'See ya, Dad!' Jamie called,
hurrying past the Late Cretaceous
model and the t-rex display. 'We're
going crabbing.'

The boys scrambled down the rocky
path from the lighthouse and ran along
the beach onto the trail that led up

20

Smuggler's Point. They bent double to catch their breath, and then clambered up the boulders to the smugglers' cave and squeezed through the gap at the back into the secret chamber.

'This is my favourite place in the whole world!' Jamie's heart began to pound as soon as he placed his feet into the fossilized dinosaur footprints on the cave floor.

'One . . . two . . . three . . . ' He counted each step. 'Keep close behind me, Tom.'

'You bet.' Tom's voice sounded excited. 'I wonder what we're going to find this time.'

'Four . . .' A crack of light appeared in the cave wall in front of him.

'Five!' The ground squelched beneath Jamie's feet and he stood blinking in the bright sunshine and breathing in the familiar warm wet-leaf smell of Dino World.

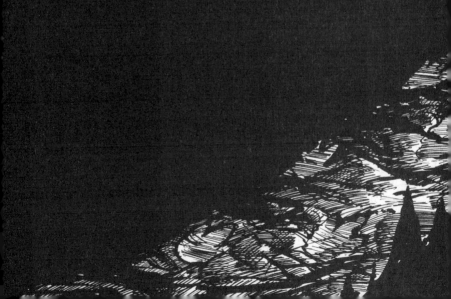

A second later, Jamie and Tom were standing on Gingko Hill, and a rough, slobbery tongue was licking Jamie's hand.

'Ready for another adventure, Wanna?' Jamie asked their little dinosaur friend.

 25

Jamie picked a stinky gingko
fruit and held it out to the
wannanosaurus.

Wanna took it gently, then
greedily gobbled it up, wagging his
tail and grunking as smelly gingko
juice dribbled down his chin.

'It's almost like he was waiting
for us,' Tom said with a laugh.

With Tom and Wanna close

behind, Jamie strode through the trees to a curtain of creepers at the edge of Gingko Hill. As he pushed the creepers aside, excitement fizzed like soda in his stomach.

Beneath them lay the steamy emerald-green jungle.

The air throbbed with the whirring
and buzzing of insects, and the jungle
rang with the strange calls of the weird
and wonderful creatures that only
lived in Dino World.

'This has got to be the best place
for adventures in the whole wide
world!' Jamie announced with a huge
grin on his face.

'In the whole solar system!'
Tom cheered.

'In the whole universe!'
Jamie exclaimed.

Wanna grunked his
agreement.

'Come on!' Jamie said. 'Let's see what we can catch in Misty Lagoon. We've only got until the tide comes in.'

The three friends clambered down the steep hillside into the dense jungle.

'We can follow the stream,' Jamie said, jumping into the shallow water that trickled and gurgled its way to the lagoon.

They splashed along the stream bed.

'That's where we met the t-rex,' Tom said, pointing to a jumble of huge rounded rocks.

'I'll never forget those fangs.' Jamie shuddered. 'I hope he's not around today.'

'Me too,' said Tom, looking round nervously. 'Let's get a move on.'

They ran until they burst out of the jungle onto the palm-fringed sandy beach of the sparkling blue lagoon.

Jamie shaded his eyes with his hand and gazed round the shore. 'Which would be the best spot to find prehistoric crabs?'

'We need deep water for crabbing,' Tom told him. 'It's no use wading into the shallows.'

'How about over there?' Jamie pointed to an outcrop of fern-covered rocks on the north-east shore. A stone ledge stuck out of the ferns like a wide diving board, hanging over the deep, blue water.

'Perfect!' Tom declared.

Jamie led the way around the lagoon to the rocks and scrambled on top of them, pushing aside the plants. It was an easy climb to the ledge over the water, and he put down his backpack in the shade of the tall ferns.

Tom scrambled up onto the ledge
next to him. 'We can't see much
through these ferns,' he said, glancing
over his shoulder. 'But Wanna will
warn us if anything tries to sneak up.'

He leaned over the lagoon and

filled up the bucket with water. 'Time to bait the line.'

Jamie knelt on the rock ledge and dug inside his backpack.

'Here's the bacon.' Jamie handed Tom a tinfoil packet and then unravelled the crab line.

Wanna watched curiously as Tom unwrapped the bacon.

'No, Wanna, it's not for you,' Tom told the little dinosaur, tearing off the bacon rind. Wanna leaned over Tom's shoulder. His long tongue shot towards the bacon.

Gak gak gak!

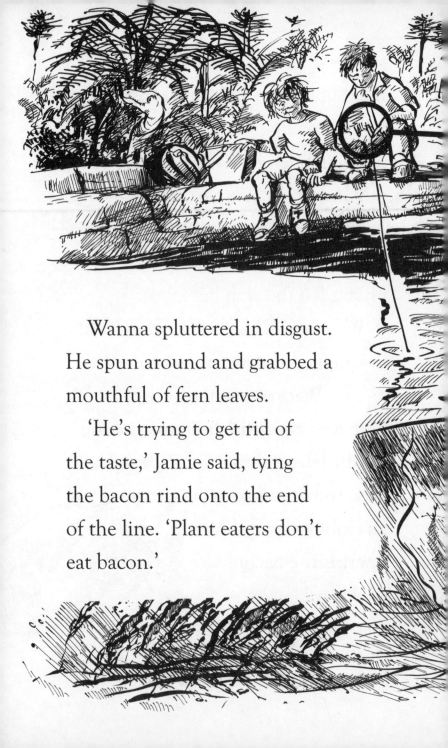

Wanna spluttered in disgust. He spun around and grabbed a mouthful of fern leaves.

'He's trying to get rid of the taste,' Jamie said, tying the bacon rind onto the end of the line. 'Plant eaters don't eat bacon.'

Tom showed Jamie how to
hold the orange plastic handle and
carefully lower the crab line into
the lagoon. Jamie felt the string run
through his fingers until the weight
came to rest on the bottom.

'Do I pull it up straight away?'
he asked.

'No.' Tom laughed. 'You have to be patient. You'll feel a tug on the line when something takes the bait.'

'What if it isn't a crab?' Jamie asked. 'What if it's a huge electric eel?'

'Ooh,' Tom said. 'What if it's a humongous stingray?'

'What if it's a Loch Ness monster with ginormous fangs?' As Jamie laughed, a big bubble broke the mirror surface of the water.

Pop!

Jamie leapt to his feet, startling Wanna, who nearly fell backwards over the bucket. But there was no giant

creature leaping out at them. The
lagoon was a calm mirror once more.

'False alarm,' Tom said. 'There's
nothing there.'

Wanna started to chew a fern
stem.

'Wanna's got the right idea,' Jamie
said. 'Let's have lunch while we wait.'

'Good idea.' Tom rummaged
in the backpack and pulled out
the tinfoil packet. He took out a
sandwich and handed it to Jamie.

'Your grandad's pickle is great!'
Tom mumbled with his mouth full.
'Even if it does blow your head off,'
he said between coughs.

'It is a bit spicy,'
Jamie agreed, taking
a huge bite. He felt
a tug on the crab
line. 'Something's
taken the bait!' he
spluttered, spraying
a mouthful of
crumbs all over
the rock. He
threw down his
sandwich and started to
pull up the line as fast as he
could. The line went limp.

Tom and Jamie peered over the
ledge. 'It got away,' Jamie realized, as

the end of the empty line came out of the water. 'It ate the bacon, too.'

'Better luck next time.' Tom tore off another strip of bacon and fixed it to the dripping line. Jamie threw it back in the water and reached for his sandwich.

'Where's my sandwich gone?' he said. There was a rustle in the ferns. Jamie whirled round in time to see the ferns stirring as a creature scurried away through them.

'Wanna!' Jamie yelled. 'You sandwich thief!'

Jamie gave the handle of the crab line to Tom and hopped off the

rock into the ferns. He could hear a
strange high-pitched rattling noise.

Ack ack ack!

'Wanna?' he called. 'Is that you?'

The ferns parted. The little
dinosaur was bobbing his head and

hopping excitedly from foot to foot. His tongue was hanging out and he was making strange noises.

Jamie knew what that meant: Wanna must have been spluttering on Grandad's pickle. 'It's your own fault. You shouldn't have stolen my sandwich,' Jamie scolded him.

'Come quick!' Tom shouted from behind him. 'We've caught something big!'

CHAPTER 3

'One, two, three . . . heave!'

Jamie and Tom pulled on the crab line with all their might.

'Look at the size of that!' Tom gasped.

43

Dangling from the crab line was the biggest crab that Jamie had ever seen. Its shell was the size of a dinner plate. The crab's silvery shell shone in the sunshine as it held tight to the bacon on the end of the line.
As Tom held the line, Jamie grabbed the bucket.

Wanna edged up and sniffed at the crab.
It waved a pincer at him.

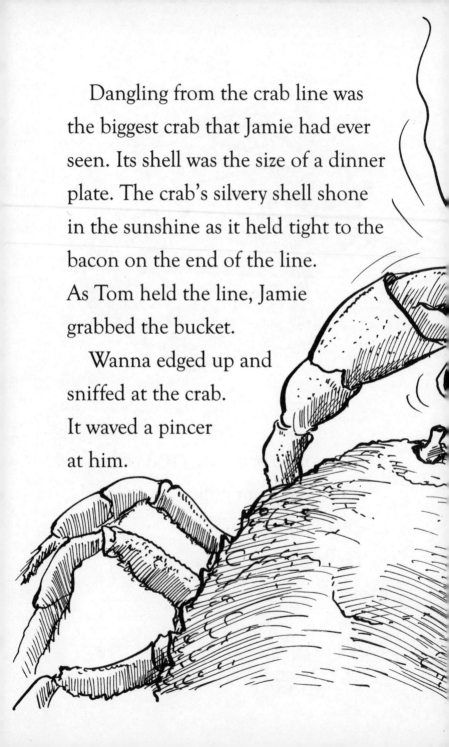

Grunk!

Wanna jumped back in alarm as Tom lowered the crab gently into the bucket.

'It's a good job this is a big bucket.'
Jamie laughed.

They peered into the bucket. The
crab was using its pincers to tear off
small pieces of the bacon
and shovel them into
its mouth.

'Crabs haven't
changed much since
dino times,' Tom
said thoughtfully.

Jamie took out
his Fossil Finder and
flipped it open. The '*HAPPY HUNTING*'
screen popped up and he tapped
CRAB into the search box. ' "*CRABS*

HAVEN'T CHANGED MUCH SINCE DINOSAUR TIMES," ' he read aloud.

Tom laughed. 'That's what I said.'

Jamie snapped shut the Fossil Finder and put it on the rock beside him. 'I want to take a close look at this dino crab,' he told Tom. 'Help me get it off the line. It's wedged in the bucket, so it shouldn't nip us.'

Tom held the bucket steady and Jamie untangled the line from the crab's pincers.

Just when he had finished, there was a sudden rustle in the ferns behind them.

Ack ack ack!

Jamie spun round to see what was
making the noise. A turkey-sized
dinosaur with open toothy jaws
dashed out from the plants onto the
ledge beside them.

Tom almost dropped
the bucket in surprise.
Snap!

The new dinosaur grabbed the Fossil Finder in its needle-sharp fangs.

Ack ack ack ack ack!

With a whip of the feathers on the end of its long yellow and orange tail, the two-legged dinosaur turned and darted into the ferns.

'What was that?' Tom said, still holding the bucket.

'Th-that . . . ' stammered Jamie, feeling the blood drain from his face, 'that was a velociraptor. A velociraptor just stole my Fossil Finder!'

Tom looked startled.

'We have to get it back,' Jamie said, shoving the crab line into his backpack.

Jamie crashed into the tall ferns and raced after the rapidly retreating raptor. Tom and Wanna plunged after him.

'It's heading towards the Far Away Mountains,' Tom said, as they emerged from the ferns into a section of the plains they hadn't been to before.

'Why did you bring the crab?' Jamie asked as they puffed along a shallow stream that flowed down to the lagoon.

Tom looked down in amazement at the bucket that swung from his hand. 'Forgot I had it,' he said. 'I'll take it back later.'

Ahead of them, the velociraptor darted into a narrow passageway where the stream gushed between two huge rocks.

'Careful,' Tom said. 'We don't know what's on the other side of the rocks.'

'Time to find out.' Jamie stepped into the cool, fast-moving stream. Edging sideways like a crab, he squeezed through the narrow gap, followed closely by Tom and Wanna.

'Wow,' he breathed. 'It's like a rainbow!'

Ahead, the stream flowed through a rocky area streaked with splashes of bright orange, yellow, and green mud and cratered with deep blue pools that sparkled in the sunshine.

'There's the raptor!' Tom pointed to a reptilian tail disappearing into a cave on the other side of the pools.

'That must be where it lives.' Jamie heaved a sigh of relief. 'Urgh!' he sputtered. 'It stinks of rotten eggs around here.'

'Wanna likes it,' Tom said, glancing at the little dinosaur. Wanna was standing next to one of the small pools with his snout in the air, sniffing deeply.

'He would,' Jamie laughed. 'He likes anything stinky.'

Wanna cocked his head to one side and peered into the pool.

'Is he looking for more crabs?'

As Tom spoke, Wanna's pool burbled and bubbled. Pop! A wisp

of hot steam escaped from a burst
bubble and the smell of rotten eggs
welled up.

'The water's hot,' Jamie chuckled.
'The only crabs he'll find in there
will be bright pink cooked ones.'

Suddenly, there was a great

whoosh!

Wanna leapt back from the pool as
a column of steaming water gushed
high into the air.

Jamie watched it, mesmerized.

'Get out of the way!' Tom

yelled as the column collapsed
and a torrent of scalding water
fell towards them.

CHAPTER 4

Jamie, Tom, and Wanna dived behind a rock as scalding drops of water rained down.

'It's a geyser,' Tom said excitedly. 'I saw one on a TV programme about Yellowstone Park. The water's heated

who

up by melted rock that bubbles up
from the centre of the earth.'

The boys and Wanna peered out
from behind the rock. On the other
side of the pools, near the raptor's
cave, there was a hissing and popping
like a champagne cork and another
geyser whooshed and spurted into
the air. Each of the six pools took

osh!

their turn to shoot jets of hot
water and steam into the air.

'No wonder that velociraptor's
chosen to live in this cave,'
murmured Tom. 'What other
dinosaur would be fast enough to run
past all the boiling geysers?'

'If we're careful, we can do it,'
Jamie said. 'We've got to get the

Whoosh!

Fossil Finder back. If we leave it
behind here, it might get fossilized—
then someone in the future could
dig up a computer next to a
dinosaur fossil. We'll just have to
learn the geysers' pattern.'

The boys watched as the geysers
repeated their eruptions.

'I think I got it,' Jamie said.

The valley had gone quiet again.

The only sound was the stream. It was as if nothing had happened.

'Now!' Tom yelled, clutching the crab bucket to his chest.

The boys and Wanna sprinted past the first pool.

Whoosh!

The huge geyser shot into the air behind them.

'Watch out!' Jamie shouted. The three jumped into the stream and hid under an overhanging rock as the hot rain pattered into the water. As soon as it had passed, Wanna darted out and dashed past the second pool and the third, dodging the bubbling water.

'Follow Wanna!' Jamie yelled to Tom, and they raced after their dinosaur friend as all around them steaming fountains of scalding water exploded from mini-geysers.

In front of the cave, an aquamarine pool began to gurgle.

'Geyser about to blow!' Tom shouted above the sound of the

fast-flowing stream. Jamie, Tom, and
Wanna sprinted past the gurgling pool
and hurled themselves behind a rock
at the edge of the cave mouth as the
last geyser exploded with
a whoosh!

Whoosh!

'That was close.' Tom
caught his breath and then
peered into the bucket. 'The
dino crab seems
to be OK.
It's waving
its pincers,
though. I
think it's
annoyed.'

'I'm not surprised.' Jamie grinned, glancing at his watch. 'We have to hurry,' he told Tom. 'It'll be high tide soon. We've got to get back before Grandad comes looking for us.'

'Sshh!' Tom whispered. 'Wanna can hear something.'

Wanna was peering into the cave with his tail sticking out stiffly behind him.

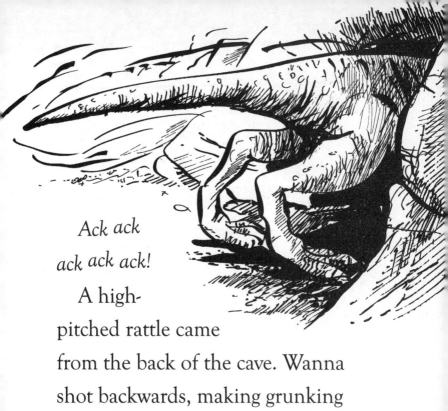

Ack ack ack ack ack!

A high-pitched rattle came from the back of the cave. Wanna shot backwards, making grunking noises.

'Hide!' Jamie hissed. The boys and Wanna ducked back behind the rock but nothing came out of the cave.

'We'll have to be careful,' Tom whispered, gently putting down the

crab bucket. 'That's the raptor's den, and animals are dangerous if you corner them in their den.'

They peered into the cave. Against the wall, near the entrance, was a

nest like a bird's, but woven from dried ferns, and the size of a car tyre. The sun was sparkling on shiny objects set among the brown stalks and leaves.

'Velociraptors must collect shiny things, like magpies,' Tom said. 'I can see the Fossil Finder!'

Jamie breathed a sigh of relief. 'It's really close and there's no sign of the raptor. He must have gone deeper into the cave. Maybe we can just grab the Fossil Finder and get out of here.'

Tom nodded. 'Let's try.'

They quietly crept into the

gloomy, dank cave and tiptoed
towards the velociraptor's
nest. Jamie's foot crunched on
something. *Ugh!* He looked down
and shuddered. Well-gnawed
bones were scattered around the
huge nest.

'It's like the nest of a giant bird of
prey,' Tom whispered from behind
him. 'If that raptor gets us, we're in
big trouble.'

A prickle of fear ran down Jamie's
spine. He knew they had to be very
careful.

Suddenly, the velociraptor shot out
of the darkness, snarling viciously.

Ack ack ack ack ack!

Jamie threw himself backwards as the raptor pounced.

Snap!

The raptor's needle-sharp teeth closed on empty air.

'Get out, quick!' Tom grabbed Jamie by the T-shirt and pulled him out of the cave and back behind the rock, nearly knocking over the dino crab bucket in the process.

Once more, they peered around the rock with Wanna grunking softly behind them.

Ack ack ack ack ack!

The velociraptor was rattling softly to itself as it bent over its nest and carefully rearranged the position of the Fossil Finder in pride of place in the centre. The whoosh of the geysers exploded down the valley, drowning out all sound.

'If we lure it out of the cave,' Jamie
whispered to Tom, 'then I can dash
in and grab the Fossil Finder.'

'We lured the ankylosaurus out
of the mud with flowers,' Tom said.
'But the velociraptor is a carnivore.'

Jamie glanced at
the crab in the bucket.
'I've got an idea!' He
rummaged in his
backpack, took out
the crab line and tied
on the remains of the
bacon.

'Cool!' Tom grinned,
taking the line. 'I've
never crabbed for
dinosaurs before.'
Tom scrambled
up onto the rocks
above the cave
and lowered the

crab line so that the bacon dangled at raptor height in the mouth of the cave.

The valley quietened again as Jamie and Wanna flattened themselves behind the rock at the side of the cave entrance. Wanna grunked softly to himself.

'We have to be patient for crabbing,' Jamie told the little dinosaur.

Suddenly, the raptor lunged out of the mouth of the cave reaching for the bacon with its sharp talons, but Tom jerked the crab line up and away. The raptor spread the

feathers on its tail and forelimbs and launched itself into the air after the meat, but it was too high.

Tom lowered the bacon again so that it was just in front of the vicious dinosaur, but pulled it away before it could grab the meat. The raptor leapt

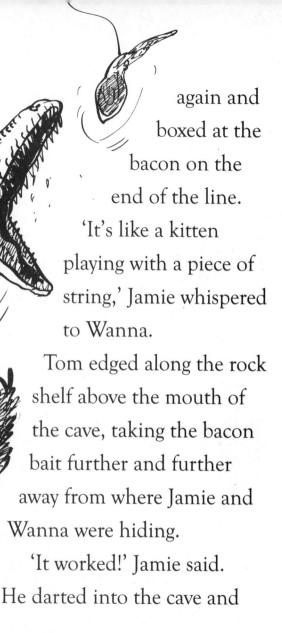

again and
boxed at the
bacon on the
end of the line.
'It's like a kitten
playing with a piece of
string,' Jamie whispered
to Wanna.

Tom edged along the rock
shelf above the mouth of
the cave, taking the bacon
bait further and further
away from where Jamie and
Wanna were hiding.

'It worked!' Jamie said.
He darted into the cave and

grabbed the Fossil Finder out of the nest. He was about to hurry away when he spotted the foil that had been wrapped around his sandwich—it had been the raptor that stole his sandwich, not Wanna!

I can't leave that to get fossilized, he thought, snatching it up. Jamie kept to the shadows and crept back the way he had come.

So far, so good, he thought, and he poked his head cautiously out of the cave.

Instead of seeing Wanna's friendly face, two cold reptilian eyes stared unblinkingly back at him.

'Oh no!' Jamie breathed.

The velociraptor was back. It tilted its head to one side.

Ack ack ack!

The raptor rattled ominously and began to twitch its tail from side to side.

Jamie's blood ran cold. It looked like a cat preparing to pounce on its prey.

Ack
ack
ack!

'It's going to attack!' Tom screamed from the ledge above as the velociraptor spread its talon-like claws and came towards Jamie.

Jamie froze to the spot. Any moment now, the raptor's sharp teeth and claws would tear him to pieces.

Something scratched at the ground behind him. Jamie whirled round. Wanna was revving up, getting a claw hold on the rock, his bony head lowered . . .

The little dinosaur charged just as the velociraptor sprang at Jamie.

Thwack!

Wanna barged into the velociraptor and bowled it over.

As the raptor spat and rattled furiously, struggling to get back to its feet, Jamie and Wanna raced behind the rock.

'Mind the crab!' Jamie yelled. Too late. Wanna's tail smacked into the bucket and knocked it over. Jamie watched as the large dino crab tumbled out, pinched its claws at him, and scuttled away. It headed towards the stream, its silvery shell

sparkling in the sunshine.

The stunned raptor stood up, shook itself, and looked around menacingly. Its tail feathers stiffened as it spotted the silvery crab scuttling past.

The raptor lunged after the crab. The crab darted this way and that as the raptor chased it.

'See! Raptors like shiny things!' Tom yelled from the ledge above the cave as the raptor turned, crouched and sprang towards the crab.

Snap!

The raptor's teeth crunched together on thin air.

87

Dino Crab hasn't got a chance,
Jamie thought, but then stared in
amazement as the crab waved its
pincers defiantly at the raptor, rushed
towards it, and pinched it on the calf
of its left leg.

Ack! The raptor leapt back in
surprise and pain.

'Go, Dino Crab!' the boys cheered,
as the crab scuttled away from the
raptor, towards the tumbling cool
stream. They watched it plop into the
water and sail like a boat downstream
towards Misty Lagoon.

The velociraptor raced after the
crab, dodging spouts of hot steam as

one after another the geysers erupted
all around it.

'Dino Crab can take care of itself.'
Tom laughed. 'That velociraptor has
met its match!'

Jamie looked at his watch. 'We
better get back,' he yelled up to Tom.

'I can see Gingko Hill from up
here,' Tom called down. 'We can go
across the plains.'

'Great!' Jamie grabbed the bucket
and he and Wanna clambered up
onto the rock ledge above the
cave. As they climbed, the
green top of Gingko Hill rose

in the distance.
'I'm glad we don't
have to go back
through the geysers.'
Wanna greeted Tom
with a wag of his tail, then
strode off along the narrow
path that led away from
the cave. At the top, Jamie
put down the bucket and
shaded his eyes to look out across
the gently rolling plains that lay

between them and Gingko Hill. On the edge of the plains, a herd of small stocky dinosaurs with big bony neck frills and parrot-like beaks was grazing peacefully on the horsetail ferns.

Jamie rummaged in his backpack and took out the Fossil Finder.

Its shiny case was dented with raptor tooth marks. He rubbed off a streak of dried raptor dribble and then flipped it open.

'It still works,' he said in relief as he typed in '*NECK FRILL*' and '*BEAK*'.

Tom looked over his shoulder. '*PROTOCERATOPS*,' he read. 'They're

harmless.' He put the crab line in the bucket and picked it up. 'And they wouldn't be browsing if any carnivores were around.'

Wanna bobbed his head as if in agreement, turned, and set off towards Gingko Hill followed by Tom. Jamie snapped the Fossil Finder shut, crammed it into his backpack, and hurried after them.

'He knows all the paths around here,' Tom said as Wanna confidently led them past the herd of peaceful protoceratops and through the jumbles of rock and tangles of tree ferns that littered the plains.

They followed the little
dinosaur across the
stream and back up
the conifer-carpeted
hillside to the top of
Gingko Hill.

Jamie checked his
watch. 'We should
make it in time to
meet Grandad,' he
said, giving Wanna
a pat on the head.
'Bye, Wanna,

see you next time. Sorry I accused you of stealing my sandwich.'

Jamie picked a handful of gingko fruit and the little dinosaur grunked happily as he settled down by his nest and began to munch on the stinky fruit.

Tom looked at his watch. 'We'll have to hurry,' he announced. The boys carefully placed their feet in the fresh dinosaur prints outside the rock face and stepped backwards out of the bright sunshine of Dino World into the darkness of the smugglers' cave. They squeezed through the gap, dashed out of the cave, and burst

out onto Smuggler's Point. Beneath them the waves were swirling close to the rocks.

'The beach will be cut off any minute,' Tom said. 'It's almost high tide.'

They sprinted down the path and reached the beach just as the first gentle waves lapped at the bottom of the pathway.

'Just in time!' Jamie shouted, as they splashed through the shallow water and hurried to the other side of the cove.

'Ahoy there, me hearties!' Grandad greeted them with a wave

from the rocks beneath Sealight Head. 'Are you ready for a crabbing adventure?'

'Just as long as there are no geysers or raptors,' Tom whispered to Jamie as they scrambled up the rocks to join him.

Jamie grinned. 'Ahoy there, Grandad,' he called. 'We're always ready for a new adventure!'

99

DINOSAUR WORLD

- - - - BOYS' ROUTE

Jungle

Misty
Lagoon

White
Ocean

100

Far Away Mountains

Crashing
Rock
Falls

Great
Plains

Gingko
Hill

GLOSSARY

Ankylosaurus (an-ki-low-sor-us) – a vegetarian dinosaur known for its armoured coat and clubbed tail. Its armour consisted of large bony bumps similar to the covering of modern-day crocodiles and lizards.

Fossil Finder – hand-held computer filled with dinosaur facts.

Geyser (gee-ser) – a hot spring, heated by volcanic activity below the earth's surface, that erupts in a tall stream of hot water and steam from time to time.

Gingko (gink-oh) – a tree native to China called a 'living fossil' because fossils of it have been found dating back millions of years, yet they are still around today. Also known as the stink bomb tree because of its smelly apricot-like fruit.

Protoceratops (pro-toh-serra-tops) – a horned, plant-eating dinosaur with a large head, neck frill

and parrot-like beak, roughly half the size of a
triceratops.

Triceratops (t-tops) (try-serra-tops) – a three-
horned, plant-eating dinosaur which looks like
a rhinoceros.

Tyrannosaurus Rex (t-rex) (ti-ran-oh-sor-us
rex) – a meat-eating dinosaur with a huge tail, two
strong legs but two tiny arms. T-rex was one of the
biggest, scariest dinosaurs.

Velociraptor (ve-loss-i-rap-tor) – meat-eating
dinosaur which was one of the smartest and fastest
dinosaurs. Velociraptors were about the size of a
turkey with a large curved claw on both of its feet.

Wannanosaurus (wah-nan-oh-sor-us) – a dinosaur
that only ate plants and used its hard, flat skull
to defend itself. Named after the place it was
discovered: Wannano in China.

Get out of my way!

I'm charging in soon . . .

Turn the page
to read the
first chapter of the
next adventure in the

Dinosaur Cove™

series:

Stampede of the
Giant Reptiles

Jamie Morgan stared at the huge
dinosaur towering over him.

'That is awesome!' he exclaimed
to his best friend Tom. 'A life-sized
model of an edmontosaurus skeleton.'

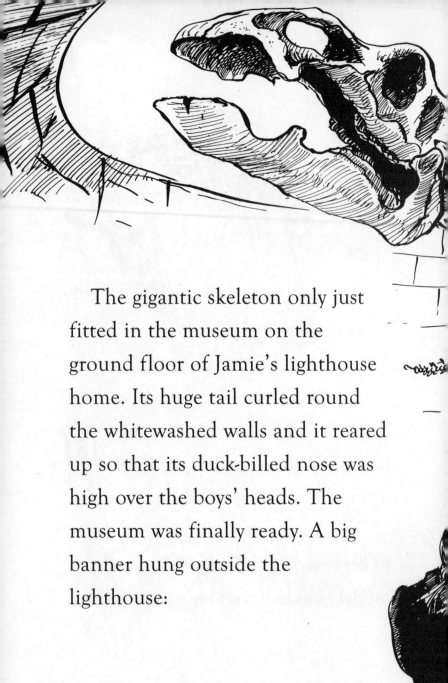

The gigantic skeleton only just
fitted in the museum on the
ground floor of Jamie's lighthouse
home. Its huge tail curled round
the whitewashed walls and it reared
up so that its duck-billed nose was
high over the boys' heads. The
museum was finally ready. A big
banner hung outside the
lighthouse:

Dinosaur Cove Museum Grand Opening Today, One O'Clock. This was the day everyone had been waiting for.

FLASH! FLASH! FLASH!

Jamie and Tom blinked in surprise. The photographer from the county paper was aiming her camera at the edmontosaurus. They jumped aside.

'It's OK, boys,' she called, waving an arm. 'Let's have you in the shot. It'll show readers just how big this beast really was.'

She took picture after picture, then grabbed Jamie's dad and made him pose over by the Cretaceous landscape model.

Tom rubbed his eyes. 'I'm seeing stars after all that!'

'But imagine how many photos she'd take if she saw a real live edmontosaurus,' said Jamie.

'We've never seen a real one close up,' said Tom.

'Maybe we will one day,' Jamie whispered.

Jamie and Tom shared an amazing secret. They had discovered Dino World, a land of living dinosaurs, and they visited it whenever they could.

'I wonder why we haven't already seen one,' said Tom.

'This will tell us where to look,' declared Jamie. He turned on his Fossil Finder and typed in: edmontosaurus.

'HERBIVORE,' he read from the screen. 'ATE LEAVES AND BRANCHES. SLOW MOVING. WALKED ON ITS BACK LEGS—just like our model.'

'But where did it live?' asked Tom.

'It says here it kept to the trees to hide from predators. That was its only defence.'

'That explains why we've never seen one,' said Tom, 'if they were always hiding. That should be our next dinosaur mission—hunt the eddie!'

Jamie put the Fossil Finder away in his backpack. He had a gleam in his eye. 'Maybe I could ask if we can have a break?'

Tom grinned. 'Are you thinking what I'm thinking?'

'Time for a trip to Dino World!'

Dad was being photographed next to the triceratops skull so Jamie and Tom ran up to Grandad. He was frowning at his reflection in a display case.

'Look at me,' he said, before Jamie had a chance to speak. 'Why can't I wear my old jumper and trousers like I do every other day of the year? I feel silly all done up like a dog's dinner.'

'But you look so smart in that suit,  Grandad,' said Jamie. 'No one will look at the exhibits. They'll all be admiring you.'

'Get away!' Grandad

laughed as he straightened his tie.
'They'll just think I'm another fossil.
Now what are you two scamps after?
Out with it.'

'It's nothing really,'
said Jamie casually.
'It's just that, well,
the museum's
ready now so we
were wondering
if we could go
outside for a while.'

Grandad looked at the
ankylosaurus-shaped clock on the
wall, showing nine fifteen. 'Don't see
why not,' he said. 'As long as you're

back sharp at one for the ceremony—clean and tidy.'

'Thanks, Grandad.' Jamie swung his backpack onto his back and hurried out of the lighthouse, Tom right behind him.

They scrambled across the beach and up to the cave entrance high in the cliffs. Making sure no one was in sight, they slipped inside. Jamie dug in his backpack for his torch, but his hand closed around something lumpy and hard.

'Hey, look,' Jamie said, pulling it out along with the torch. 'This is the ammonite I found on my first day in Dinosaur Cove.'

'The first day we discovered Dino World,' Tom remembered.

Jamie tossed the fossil in his backpack and shone the torch on the five fossilized footprints in the stone floor. Every time he saw them he felt the same rush of excitement.

'Let's get back there,' he said. The boys trod in each of the dinosaur prints. One ... two ... three ... four ... FIVE! The dark cave disappeared and they stepped into the scorching heat and dazzling light of Dino World.

'It's great to be back!' exclaimed Tom, looking at the huge trees and dense jungle undergrowth around them.

Instead of the usual hum of insects and distant calls of dinosaurs there was an eerie silence.

'Listen!' Jamie said.

Tom listened hard. 'I can't hear a thing.'

'Exactly,' said Jamie. 'Something's not right.'

'Wanna!' called Jamie. His voice sounded strange, echoing through the silent trees. 'Where are you, Wanna?'

There was no sign of the friendly little dinosaur who usually came to greet them. The boys began searching the undergrowth, pushing aside giant tangled creepers.

There was a rustling in a nearby laurel bush. 'What was that?' Jamie stopped. 'Wanna?'

The little wannanosaurus crept out from between the leaves, his eyes darting about nervously. Jamie and Tom rushed over and hugged him.

'You don't know how pleased we
are to see you,' said Tom, scratching
him hard on his scaly back.

But Wanna just gave a feeble grunk.

Tom frowned. 'This isn't like you,
Wanna. What's the matter?'

Jamie reached up into a tree and picked some orange fruit. 'I know what you need, boy,' he said. He tossed one to Wanna and put the others in his backpack.

Wanna looked warily around and then gulped the fruit.

'One thing hasn't changed,' said Jamie. 'Wanna still loves gingkoes.'

'Another thing hasn't changed,' Tom said, holding his nose. 'The gingkoes are still as smelly as ever.'

'But everything else is different.' Jamie frowned. 'Let's find out what's going on.'

Join Jamie and Tom
in Dino World
with the

Dinosaur Cove™

CRETACEOUS SURVIVAL GUIDE

Turn the page for a taster
of all the awesome
things to do . . .

Create!

MAKE YOUR OWN
EDIBLE DINO POO!

YOU WILL NEED:
- 100g plain chocolate
- 50g margarine
- 2 tablespoons golden syrup
- 150g plain digestive biscuits

Don't forget to ask a grown-up to help melt the chocolate!

1 Put the biscuits in a large freezer bag and tie the bag shut. Using a rolling pin, bash the biscuits into crumbs.

2 Break up the chocolate into pieces and put them in a saucepan. Heat the pan on a low temperature until the chocolate has melted.

3 Stir the margarine and syrup into the melted chocolate.

4 Take the saucepan off the heat. Pour the biscuit crumbs into the chocolate mixture and stir together.

36

37

Play!

WHICH CRETACEOUS DINO ARE YOU?

START
Do you walk on two legs or four legs?

Two legs — Super speedy or supremely strong?

Four legs — Super speedy or supremely strong?

Super speedy or supremely strong? — Carnivore or herbivore?

Hunt on land or in the air?

Up high or down low?

Protected by horns or bony armour?

Land — T-Rex
Quetzalcoatlus
Velociraptor
Wannanosaurus

Down low — Bagaceratops
Up high — Edmontosaurus
Horns — Triceratops
Bony armour — Ankylosaurus

Discover!

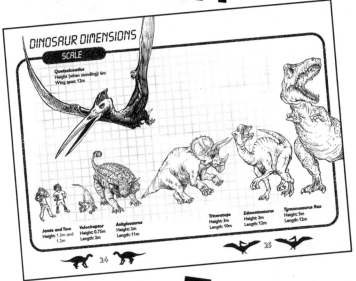

DINOSAUR DIMENSIONS

SCALE

Quetzalcoatlus
Height (when standing): 6m
Wing span: 12m

Jamie and Tom
Height: 1.3m and
1.2m

Velociraptor
Height: 0.75m
Length: 2m

Ankylosaurus
Height: 2m
Length: 11m

Triceratops
Height: 3m
Length: 10m

Edmontosaurus
Height: 3m
Length: 12m

Tyrannosaurus Rex
Height: 5m
Length: 12m

Explore!

T-REX: THE LIZARD KING

Tyrannosaurus Rex was a carnivore that ate all sorts of other creatures, from small dinosaurs like velociraptors to large ones like edmontosaurs. Palaeontologists think the t-rex was probably a scavenger as well as a hunter, eating up the remains of creatures that had already died. With chisel-shaped teeth at the front and huge teeth with knife-like serrated edges filling the rest of its mouth, the t-rex was a fearsome predator. The biggest t-rex skull ever found is 150cm long and was discovered in the 1960s. The biggest and best preserved whole t-rex skeleton is in the Field Museum of Natural History in Chicago. Its name is FMNH PR 2081, but its nickname is Sue.

We found out that competition for food was fierce in the Cretaceous period when we ran into not one but two t-rexes! We'd only just managed to escape one dino's snapping jaws when we stumbled into a battle between two of the massive lizard kings.